Basketball Stars

Therese Shea

Children's Press®
A Division of Scholastic Inc.
New York / Toronto / London / Auckland / Sydney
Mexico City / New Delhi / Hong Kong
Danbury, Connecticut

Book Design: Dean Galiano
Contributing Editor: Karl Bollers

Photo Credits: Cover © Gregory Shamus/Getty Images; p. 4 © Jeff Haynes/AFP/
Getty Images; p. 6 © Jonathan Daniel/Getty Images; pp. 8, 27, 32 © Lisa Blumenfled/
Getty Images; pp. 12, 15, 19, 24, 39 © AP/Wide World Photos; p. 17 © Mike Nolan/
Getty Images; p. 20 © Stephen Dunn/Getty Images; p. 31 © Paul Buck/AFP/Getty
Images; p. 37 © Mark Dadswell/Getty Images.

Library of Congress Cataloging-in-Publication Data

Shea, Therese.
    Basketball stars / Therese Shea.
    p. cm.—(Greatest sports heroes)
    Includes index.
    ISBN-10: 0-531-12584-X (lib. bdg.)   0-531-18701-2 (pbk.)
    ISBN-13: 978-0-531-12584-7 (lib. bdg.)   978-0-531-18701-2 (pbk.)
    1. Basketball players—United States—Biography—Juvenile literature.
    I. Title. II. Series.
    GV884.A1S457 2007
    796.3230922-dc22
    [B]
                                                2006015125

2 3 4 5 6 7 8 9 10 R 11 10 09 08 07

Contents

Introduction

There are only seconds left in the game. The clock is ticking and your team is down by one point. You have the basketball. You quickly pass it to your teammate. The players race down the court. Your teammate aims for the basket. Immediately, defenders are waving their hands in his face, blocking his shot. He looks around. You make eye contact. You weave between defenders and find yourself open. Your teammate passes the ball. You grab hold of it, jump, and spin while aiming for the rim. The crowd holds its breath as you release the ball. The ball goes into the net as the clock turns to zero. Swish! Two points! Your team wins!

Basketball is a very exciting sport. It consists of two teams of five players who are in constant motion. Each team attempts to score more baskets than the other team. Each team also tries to stop the opposing team from scoring.

Former Chicago Bulls shooting guard Michael Jordan is considered by many to be the greatest professional basketball player of all time.

Basketball star Shaquille O'Neal is so popular that his career has crossed over into movies, music, and even video games.

Players have different positions on the court. There are usually two guards, two forwards, and a center. Guards are skilled at passing, dribbling, and shooting. Forwards usually shoot and grab rebounds close to the basket. A rebound is when a player grabs a ball after it has bounced off the rim of the basket or the backboard. Centers usually work closer to the basket, taking short shots, blocking shots, and rebounding. They are usually the tallest people on the team.

One characteristic all these players have in common is the knowledge that it takes an entire team to win a basketball game. Let's meet some of today's best basketball players.

"Hopefully, I can become a staple, like my teammate Shaq. I'm grateful that NBA fans think so highly of my game."

—*Dwyane Wade*

Miami Heat guard Dwyane Wade has earned the nickname "Flash." Besides being fast, Dwyane is a fine shooter and passer. His quick hands get him many assists. An assist is a pass that results in a goal. At 6 feet (2 meters) 4 inches (10 centimeters), Dwyane is small compared to other pro players, but he has quickly become one of the best in the National Basketball Association (NBA).

Dwyane was born on January 17, 1982, in Chicago. He first played basketball on a team coached by his father. Dwyane was always a good rebounder but had to work hard to master other aspects of the game. He was accepted at Marquette University and joined their team. In

Miami fans go wild as Dwyane Wade scores in a game against the Los Angeles Lakers.

his first two years, he averaged 19.7 points and set a Marquette single-season scoring record of 710 points. Dwyane received a lot of attention during the 2003 National Collegiate Athletic Association (NCAA) tournament. He was the third player in NCAA tournament history to have a triple-double. A triple-double is when a player scores double-digits in three categories during a single game. Marquette went on to the Final Four, the last four teams remaining in the NCAA play-offs, for the first time since 1977.

Dwyane was the 2003 Conference USA Player of the Year as well as Defensive Player of the Year. He received the Marquette Most Valuable Player (MVP) award and the sportsmanship award. After such an amazing

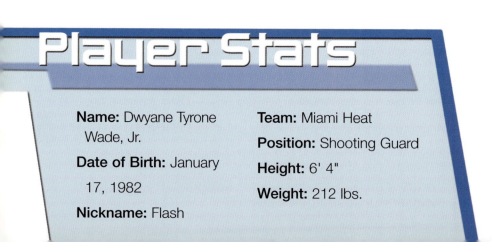

Player Stats

Name: Dwyane Tyrone Wade, Jr.

Date of Birth: January 17, 1982

Nickname: Flash

Team: Miami Heat

Position: Shooting Guard

Height: 6' 4"

Weight: 212 lbs.

season, Dwyane felt ready to enter the professional basketball world. He was selected fifth overall in the 2003 NBA draft by the Miami Heat. A draft is a system by which new players are selected for professional sports teams.

In sixty-one games of the 2003–2004 NBA season, Dwyane averaged 16.2 points. This average was a Miami rookie record. Dwyane was voted to the NBA All-Rookie First Team. Dwyane also helped the Heat reach the 2004 playoffs.

In the 2004–2005 season, star center Shaquille O'Neal joined the Miami Heat. He and Dwyane helped take the Heat to the play-offs again. In the 2005 play-offs, Dwyane averaged 26.3 points, 8.8 assists, and 6 rebounds while making half of the shots he attempted. Only seven other NBA players have ever done this and all of them are in the Basketball Hall of Fame!

Dwyane is a real family man. He is married and has a son. In addition, Dwyane donates tickets for each Miami Heat home game to children's organizations.

"I'm like a superhero. Call me Basketball Man."
—LeBron James

LeBron James is often called a phenomenon. He has been amazing fans, coaches, and teammates since he was a freshman in high school. Now he is amazing NBA fans.

LeBron was born in Akron, Ohio, on December 30, 1984. LeBron had an immediate impact as a point guard on his high school basketball team. The team had a perfect 27-0 record that season and won the state championship.

In his second year, when his school again won the state title, LeBron was named "Mr. Basketball" of Ohio. He was the first high school sophomore to be named to the USA Today All-USA First Team. He also received this honor as a junior and a senior. LeBron was the 2003 National High School Player of

Cleveland Cavaliers' LeBron James is one of the youngest, most gifted players currently in the NBA.

the Year. He decided to enter the 2003 NBA draft and was picked first overall by the Cleveland Cavaliers.

Could LeBron deliver? He answered the question by being named Eastern Conference Rookie of the Month every month of his first NBA season. LeBron showed great scoring ability, but also rare "court vision." He can anticipate where his teammates and opponents will be and call plays that result in baskets.

Young Gun

LeBron went on to become the youngest NBA player to score a triple-double and the youngest player to score 2,000 points. For the

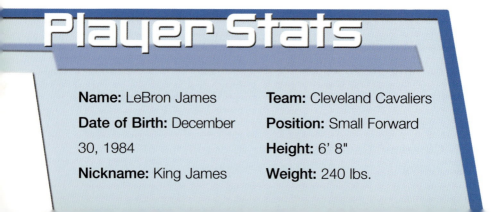

Player Stats

Name: LeBron James

Date of Birth: December 30, 1984

Nickname: King James

Team: Cleveland Cavaliers

Position: Small Forward

Height: 6' 8"

Weight: 240 lbs.

2005–2006 season, Cleveland added new players, new coaches, and a new winning attitude. LeBron led the Cavaliers to the 2006 playoffs, where the team performed very well. LeBron and his teammates took the powerful Detroit Pistons to game seven of the Eastern Conference Semifinals.

Will LeBron and Cleveland capture a championship? If LeBron gets his chance, you can bet they will!

Net Works

James Naismith, a Canadian physical education teacher, invented basketball in 1891. Naismith, assisted by Luther Halsey Gulick, first wrote up rules in 1892 at Springfield College in Massachusetts. In the beginning, players dribbled a soccer ball and shot it into a peach basket! An open-ended net was introduced about ten years later.

Chapter Three

Lauren Jackson

*"I definitely aspire to be the best ever—
definitely—and that's been my goal since I
was, well, born."*

—Lauren Jackson

Lauren Jackson's interest in basketball is no
surprise. Her parents played on Australian
national basketball teams and Lauren started
playing basketball at age four. She grew up to
dominate women's basketball on two continents!

Lauren Jackson was born May 11, 1981,
in Albury, New South Wales, Australia. As
a teenager, she was asked to attend the
esteemed Australian Institute of Sport in
Canberra, Australia. Lauren took the Institute's
basketball team to two championships in the
Australian Women's National Basketball
League. At sixteen, she was also the youngest
player ever to join the Australian women's
national basketball team. A year later, Lauren

With Lauren Jackson on the team, Australia's Price
Attack Opals beat the United States team in the Opal
World Challenge match.

helped Australia win the bronze medal at the 1998 World Championships.

Lauren represented Australia in the 2000 Summer Olympics. She then joined the professional team Canberra Capitals in 2000. With Lauren's help, the Capitals won the championship for the next three years.

Lauren decided to play each summer for the Women's National Basketball Association (WNBA) in the United States. In the 2001 WNBA draft, the Seattle Storm picked Lauren first overall.

In Lauren's first year with the Storm, she led her team and all other rookies in points, rebounds, steals, and blocks. She was named an all-star and finished in second place for Rookie of the Year.

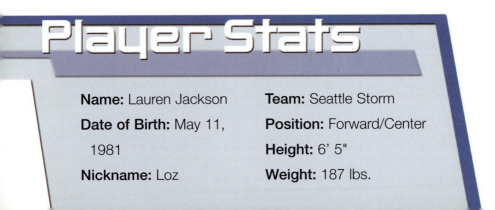

Player Stats

Name: Lauren Jackson

Date of Birth: May 11, 1981

Nickname: Loz

Team: Seattle Storm

Position: Forward/Center

Height: 6' 5"

Weight: 187 lbs.

Muriel Page of the Washington Mystics tries to block Lauren as she attempts to pass the ball to a Seattle Storm teammate.

For the 2002 season, Lauren was again named to the WNBA All-Star team for the Western Conference. In 2003, she led the WNBA in scoring and was named WNBA MVP. She was the first international player and the youngest to ever win this award.

Lauren aggravated an old leg injury when she returned to Australia to play in the 2005–2006 season. After a swift recovery, Lauren decided to leave the Capitals and signed to play with a South Korean team.

Chapter Four

Tim Duncan

"I'm still learning. Hopefully I can keep getting better, and not stop where I am now."

—Tim Duncan

Tim Duncan is different from many NBA players. He did not grow up playing basketball in a big city. He was born on Saint Croix in the U.S. Virgin Islands on April 25, 1976. When Tim was young, he dreamed of becoming an Olympic swimmer like his sister Tricia. However, in 1989, Hurricane Hugo destroyed his team's pool. When swim practice moved to the ocean, Tim's fear of sharks kept him from attending.

Tim's brother-in-law, Ricky, believed he saw a natural basketball talent in Tim and taught him some basic skills. Tim began to play at his high school. People began to notice his quick feet and natural ability. During Tim's senior year, he averaged 25 points, 12 rebounds,

Tim Duncan attempts to get past the furious defense of the Los Angeles Lakers during a March 2006 game.

and 5 blocks per game. Word of his skill spread to the United States and Dave Odom, head coach of Wake Forest University in North Carolina, traveled to Saint Croix to see Tim. When Odom asked him to play for the Wake Forest Demon Deacons, Tim agreed.

At the start of his freshman year at Wake Forest, Tim had difficulty scoring. His defensive skills were still strong, though. Coach Odom knew that Tim needed time to gain confidence. In 1995, Tim led Wake Forest to win the Atlantic Coast Conference (ACC) tournament and to the final sixteen teams of the NCAA tournament. The National Association of Basketball Coaches (NABC) named him Defensive Player of the Year. He received this award again in the next two years. In the 1995–1996 season, Wake Forest

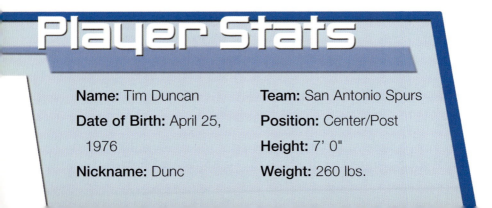

Player Stats

Name: Tim Duncan

Date of Birth: April 25, 1976

Nickname: Dunc

Team: San Antonio Spurs

Position: Center/Post

Height: 7' 0"

Weight: 260 lbs.

again won the ACC conference championships and made it to the final eight teams in the NCAA tournament.

A Good Son

Tim could have joined the NBA after his junior year of college, but he had promised his mother he would complete his degree. Although Wake Forest was ranked as the second team in the nation, they did not win the ACC or the NCAA tournament his final year. Still, Tim was the first player in NCAA history to reach 1,500 points, 1,000 rebounds, 400 blocked shots, and 200 assists. He won the 1997 John Wooden Award for best overall player and was named the Naismith College Player of the Year. The Naismith awards are named for basketball's inventor.

The Big Show

Tim Duncan, now 7 feet (2 m) tall, was chosen first overall in the 1997 NBA draft by the San Antonio Spurs. That season, the Spurs reached the second round of the NBA

Fans are riveted by the exciting game play as Tim faces off against the Lakers' Karl Malone.

play-offs and Tim was named Rookie of the Year. The following season, the Spurs won the NBA Championship for the first time ever. Tim took the award for Finals MVP.

The next three seasons Tim and the Spurs performed well in the regular season. Tim was named the 2002 NBA MVP. San Antonio made it once again to the NBA Finals in 2003. Tim finished the series with a record-breaking 32 blocks and the Spurs won the NBA Championship. Tim received the Finals MVP award as well as the league MVP award. The Spurs won the championship again at the end of the 2004–2005 season. Tim was the Finals MVP for the third time!

Tim is the "complete package." He is a great player on the court and a great role model off the court. Tim focuses on many charities such as the Tim Duncan Foundation.

"For the most part I try to stay focused not on my play, but on our team."

—Steve Nash

Steve Nash worked hard for success. In 2005, the hard work paid off when this point guard was named the NBAs MVP. Steve was born February 7, 1974, in Johannesburg, South Africa. His father was a professional soccer player. The family soon moved to Vancouver Island, British Columbia, in Canada. Steve grew up excelling in many sports. In high school, he was named British Columbia Player of the Year in soccer, but decided to pursue basketball instead.

By his senior year of high school, Steve had proven himself an extraordinary point guard. He was lightning fast and had a great jump shot. Most U.S. colleges, however, were not interested in this unknown Canadian player.

Phoenix Suns' point guard Steve Nash races up court during the 2006 NBA play-offs.

Then Santa Clara University coach Dick Davey saw Steve play and he saw a future star. Steve promised to play for the Santa Clara Broncos.

A Ticket to the Big Dance

Coach Davey was not disappointed. The Santa Clara Broncos won the 1993 West Coast Conference (WCC) Tournament. Steve was the first freshman ever named WCC Tournament MVP. The Broncos also won the chance to play in the NCAA Tournament and became the first number fifteen seed to defeat a number two seed. A seed is a rank in a tournament based on previous records. In the last 31 seconds of the 64-61 win, Steve made 6 straight free throws.

Player Stats

Name: Steven John Nash

Date of Birth: February 7, 1974

Nickname: Kid Canadian

Team: Phoenix Suns

Position: Point Guard

Height: 6' 1"

Weight: 195 lbs.

In his junior year, he was named WCC Player of the Year, an honor he received again after his senior year. In the 1996 NBA draft, the Phoenix Suns picked Steve fifteenth overall. Unfortunately, Steve did not play a big role with the Suns during his first two years. He was traded to the Dallas Mavericks in 1998. His first season with them was a disappointment. The next two seasons were much better. In the 2000–2001 season, *Basketball Digest* named him "Comeback Player of the Year." His team went to the play-offs for the first time in a decade, but they lost in the second round to the San Antonio Spurs.

The Big Three

The next two seasons were even better for Steve and the Mavericks. Steve and forwards Dirk Nowitzki and Michael Finley became known as the Big Three for their scoring power. Dallas made it to the Western Conference Finals in 2003.

After Dallas lost in the first round of the play-offs in 2004, they did not renew Steve's contract, an official written agreement. They feared he was becoming too old. The Phoenix Suns, however, felt differently. Steve's former team wanted him as their leader.

The 2004–2005 season was the best of Steve's career. When Steve got the ball, his teammates raced with him down the court. The result was the highest scoring NBA team in over ten years and fast-paced basketball that was exciting to watch.

Steve was named 2005 NBA MVP. His unselfish style of play made him a leader in

Net Works

Wheelchair basketball was first played in the United States by World War II (1939–1945) veterans. In 1949, six teams established the National Wheelchair Basketball Association (NWBA). A dribble rule was added in 1964 to bounce the ball twice on alternating sides of the wheelchair. In 1993, the International Wheelchair Basketball Federation (IWBF) was established as the governing body. Today, the IWBF oversees wheelchair basketball tournaments in countries all around the world.

From 1999 to 2004, Steve brought his talents to the Dallas Mavericks before eventually being traded back to the Suns.

assists rather than points. Showing he is a team player, Steve asked his teammates to accept the MVP award with him.

Steve makes valuable contributions both on the court and off. In 2001, he set up the Steve Nash Foundation to help poor kids with education, health, and personal growth. He has shown that one player can raise a team to a whole new level.

Chapter Six

Kevin Garnett

"We have to do the impossible, but it's possible."
—*Kevin Garnett*

Born May 19, 1976, Kevin Garnett practically grew up on the basketball court. Kevin's high school career began in Mauldin, South Carolina. He was named South Carolina's "Mr. Basketball" after his junior year. He moved to Chicago the next year. During his senior year at Farragut Academy, he averaged 25.2 points, 17.9 rebounds, 6.7 assists, and 6.5 blocks. With these amazing numbers, he was voted "Mr. Basketball" of Illinois, as well as *USA Today*'s 1995 National High School Player of the Year. Kevin became the first player drafted out of high school in twenty years.

The Minnesota Timberwolves picked Kevin fifth overall in the 1995 NBA draft. Although Kevin was not an explosive scorer in his rookie year, his defense was impressive.

Los Angeles Clippers' Chris Kaman gives it his all, but he is no match for the Timberwolves' Kevin Garnett.

First-Time All-Star

In the 1996–1997 season, Kevin was named an all-star for the first time. The Timberwolves also went to the play-offs for the first time. In January 1998, Kevin scored his first triple-double with 18 points, 13 rebounds, and 10 assists in a win against Denver. He was also picked as a starter for the 1998 All-Star Game.

Starting with the 1999–2000 season, Kevin began a streak, averaging more than 20 points, 10 rebounds, and 5 assists per game. He currently holds the record for the most consecutive seasons achieving these numbers. At the 2003 All-Star Game, he was named MVP after recording 37 points, 9 rebounds, 5 steals, and 3 assists.

Player Stats

Name: Kevin Garnett

Date of Birth: May 19, 1976

Nickname: The Big Ticket

Team: Minnesota
Timberwolves

Position: Power Forward/
Center

Height: 6' 11"

Weight: 240 lbs.

The 2003–2004 season was Kevin's best season yet. He averaged 24.2 points, 2.17 blocks, and 13.9 rebounds per game. This was the highest number of rebounds and points in the league. The Timberwolves ended with the best record in the Western Conference. Kevin was named the 2004 NBA MVP.

Kevin continues to be a superstar on the court. He has played in every All-Star Game since his second season. He continues to chase his dream of an NBA championship title.

Good for the Kids

Kevin enjoys working with students through the For Excellence in Leadership Foundation.This organization connects high school and college students with business leaders to prepare them for success in their future careers. Kevin was given the November 2005 NBA Community Assist Award.

"I really don't care about scoring as long as we win…that's all that gets us going, is winning."
—Diana Taurasi

Diana Taurasi is the most exciting addition to WNBA basketball in recent years. She was born in Chino, California, on June 11, 1982. Her parents are from Argentina where her father was a professional soccer player.

Diana first made heads turn playing basketball at Don Lugo High School. She ended her high school career with 3,047 points, the second highest in state history. She was named the 2000 ESPN Scholastic Sports America Player of the Year. Diana was also the 2000 Naismith Female Prep National Player of the Year. After high school, Diana decided to attend the University of Connecticut.

Diana joined the Huskies and was named the 2001 Big East Championship's Most

Diana Taurasi understands the true concept of teamwork as she looks for an open teammate to pass the ball to.

Outstanding Player. She was the first rookie to receive this honor. Over the next three years, the Huskies won the national championship three times! Diana won the Naismith National Player of the Year award in 2003 and 2004.

Diana was picked first overall by the Phoenix Mercury in the 2004 WNBA draft. She was named 2004 WNBA Rookie of the Year. Diana was also selected to the U.S. women's national basketball team for the 2004 Summer Olympics in Athens, Greece. She was the youngest player on the team and averaged 8.5 points in about 19 minutes of play per game. The U.S. won the gold medal.

Player Stats

Name: Diana Taurasi

Date of Birth: June 11, 1982

Nickname: Dee

Team: Phoenix Mercury

Position: Guard/Forward

Height: 6' 0"

Weight: 172 lbs.

Diana goes toe-to-toe with an opponent during the 2004 NCAA Women's Final Four.

Diana focuses on being part of a super team. With WNBA career game highs of 31 points and 11 rebounds in the 2005 season, she continues to raise her team to championship levels. Diana is inspiring a new generation of women to achieve athletic greatness.

Net Works

An increased interest in women's college basketball led to the creation of a women's professional league. The WNBA started in June 1997. Sheryl Swoopes was the first player to sign a contract with a WNBA team. Cynthia Cooper was named the first WNBA MVP. Lisa Leslie was the first WNBA player to be named regular season WNBA MVP, All-Star MVP, and MVP of the WNBA Championships all in one season.

Keep an eye on future NBA star Chris James. Chris was selected the 2005-2006 NBA Rookie of the Year. Here he is in action for his college team, Wake Forest.

New Words

assist (uh-**sist**) a pass that results in a goal

contract (kon-**trakt**) an official written agreement between two or more people or groups

draft (**draft**) a system by which new players are selected for professional sports teams

dribble (**drib**-uhl) to bounce a ball repeatedly while running, keeping it under control

Final Four (**fye**-nuhl **for**) the last four teams remaining in the NCAA playoff tournament

free throw (**free throh**) an unguarded shot taken from the foul line by a player whose opponent committed a foul

New Words

jump shot (**juhmp shot**) a shot where the player jumps into the air and releases the ball at the highest point of the jump

phenomenon (fe-nom-uh-**non**) something or someone very unusual and remarkable

rebound (**ree**-bound) act of grabbing the ball after it has bounced off the rim of the basket or the backboard

seed (**seed**) a rank in a tournament that is based on previous records

triple-double (**trip**-uhl-**duh**-buhl) when a player scores double-digits in three categories during a single game

For Further Reading

Jackel, Molly, and Joe Layden. *WNBA Superstars*. New York: Scholastic, Inc., 1998.

Nelson, Glenn, Dalton Ross, and Andrea Whittaker. *Rising Stars: The Ten Best Young Players in the NBA*. New York: The Rosen Publishing Group, Inc., 2002.

Paul, Alan, and Jon Kramer. *Basketball All-Stars: The NBA's Best*. New York: The Rosen Publishing Group, Inc., 2002.

Weatherspoon, Teresa, Tara Sullivan, and Kelly Whiteside. *Teresa Weatherspoon's Basketball for Girls*. Hoboken, NJ: John Wiley and Sons, 1999.

Resources

ORGANIZATIONS

Naismith Memorial Basketball Hall of Fame
1000 West Columbus Avenue
Springfield, MA 01105
Phone: (413) 781-6500 or (877) 4HOOPLA
www.hoophall.com

**National Basketball Association/
Women's National Basketball Association**
Olympic Tower, 645 Fifth Avenue
New York, NY 10022
Phone: (212) 688-9622
FanRelations@NBA.com

Women's Basketball Hall of Fame
700 Hall of Fame Drive
Knoxville, TN 37915
Phone: (865) 633-9000
www.wbhof.com

Resources

WEB SITES

International Wheelchair Basketball Federation

www.iwbf.org/

This site has the latest news on wheelchair basketball along with information on the IWBF and links to related Web sites.

National Basketball Association

www.nba.com

This official site of the NBA provides the latest news in the world of professional basketball along with schedules, scores, player stats, bios, and cool videos.

Women's National Basketball Association

www.wnba.com

This official site of the WNBA provides the latest news in the world of women's basketball along with schedules, scores, player stats, bios, and cool videos.

Index

Index

ABOUT THE AUTHOR

Therese Shea lives and writes in Buffalo, New York. A graduate of Providence College and the State University of New York at Buffalo, she is the author of several books.